W

PENGUIN WORKSHOP
An Imprint of Penguin Random House LLC, New York

Copyright © 2021 by Jonathan Fenske. All rights reserved. Published by Penguin Workshop, an imprint of
Penguin Random House LLC, New York. PENGUIN and PENGUIN WORKSHOP are trademarks of Penguin Books Ltd,
and the W colophon is a registered trademark of Penguin Random House LLC. Manufactured in China.

Visit us online at www.penguinrandomhouse.com.

Library of Congress Cataloging-in-Publication Data is available upon request.

ISBN 9781524793104   10 9 8 7 6 5 4 3 2 1

Something Stinks!

by Jonathan Fenske

Penguin Workshop

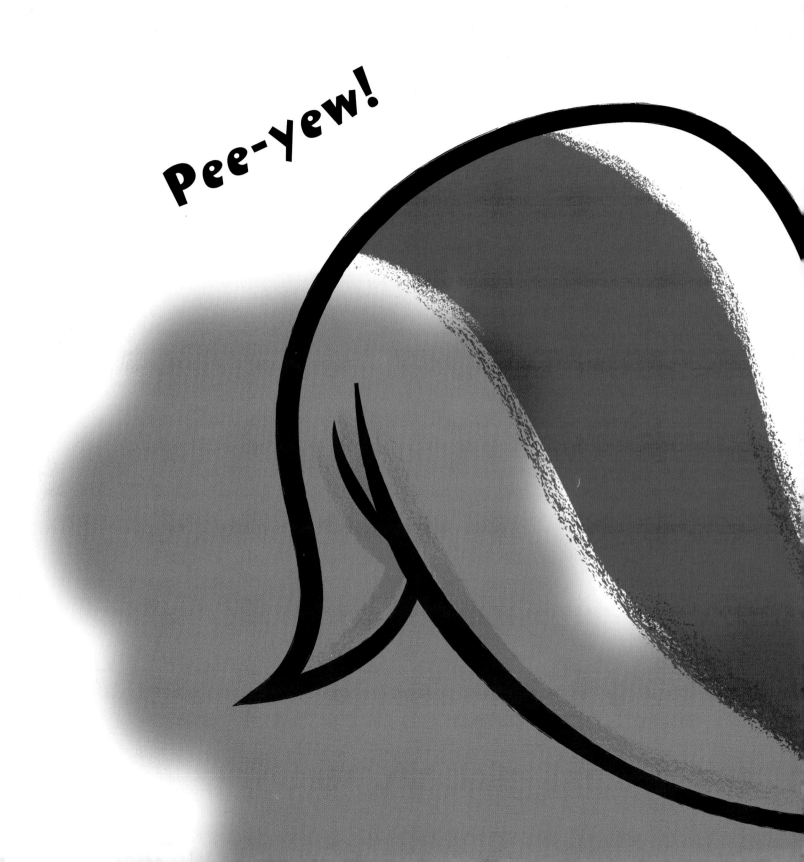

Something STINKS!

Can you smell that?
No?
Well, you sure are LUCKY.

It is stinkier than sweaty, dirty, crusty socks that have been at the bottom of the laundry basket **FOR A WHOLE WEEK.**

Super stinky!

You get the idea.
But don't worry.

Your good friend Skunk will find out
where this terrible stench is coming from!

I will look in every corner!

I will look in every crack!

Aha! It must be . . .

UNDERPANTS!

Rats! These underpants are nice and fresh.

Wonderful.

Now the smell is
getting WORSE.

Like someone or some**THING**
has been dragging a great big
cloud of stink everywhere!

Hmmm. I don't mean
to be rude, but do you
think it could be YOU?

Ugh. I think I am going to be sick.

Please, please, **PLEASE**, if you see
something stinky, let me know.

What's that?
You **DO** see something stinky?

Where is it?
WHERE?

I see you pointing.

I hear you shouting.

I DON'T UNDERSTAND WHAT YOU'RE TRYING TO TELL ME!

Aaack! Forget it!
I can't take any more!

THE STINK WINS!

Hmmm. That's weird.
NOW it smells MUCH better!

Whatever could have been so stinky?

Oh, well.

I guess we'll
never know.